Caterpillar Yom Kippur

by Jennifer Tzivia MacLeod

ISBN-13: 978-1988976006 (Safer Editions)
ISBN-10: 1988976006

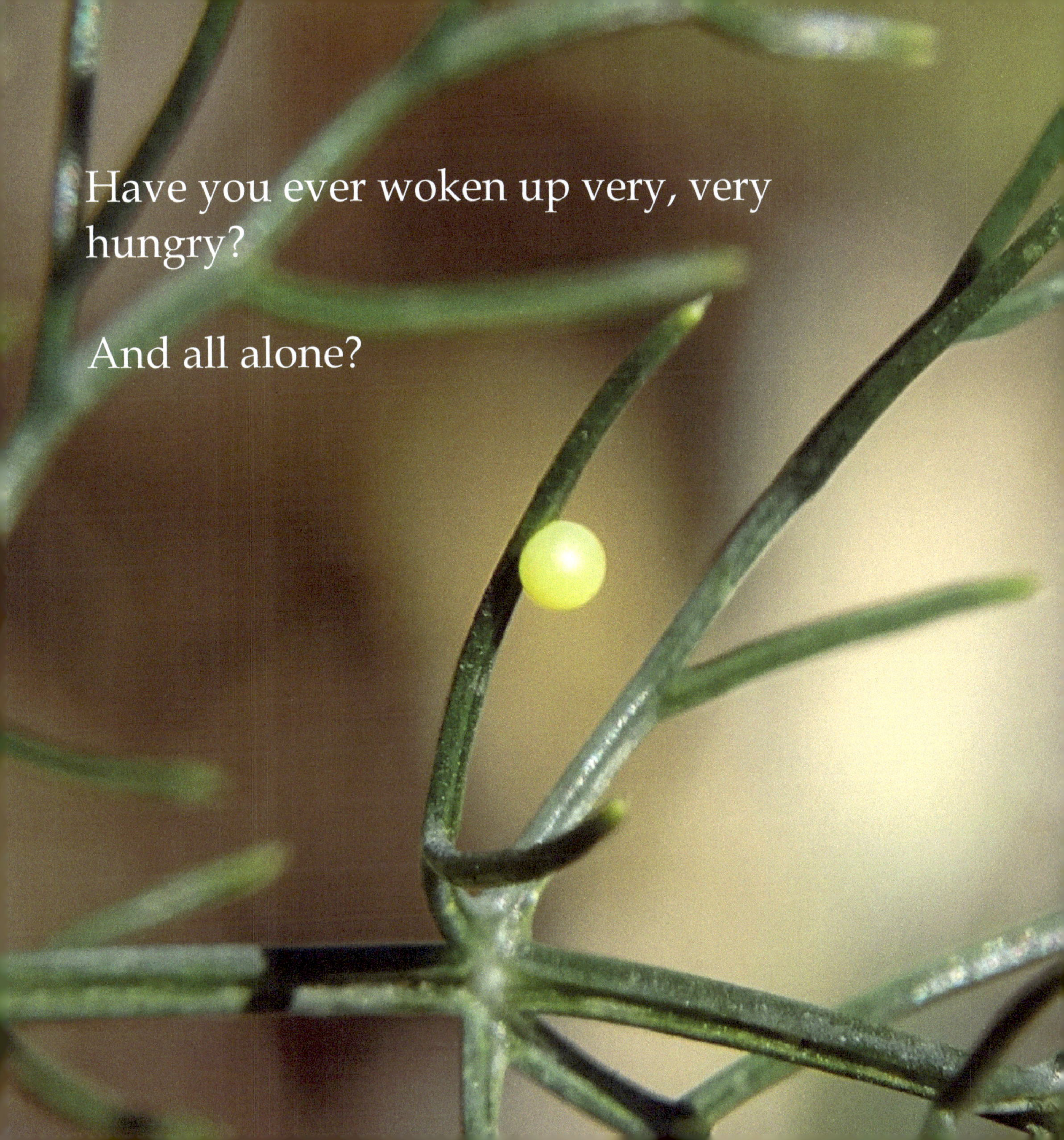

Have you ever woken up very, very hungry?

And all alone?

All you can think about is what you're going to eat.

And maybe how to find a friend.

It's a lot of work, growing and changing every single day.

Delicious work.

But sometimes you start to wonder.

Yom Kippur is a day to stop eating and start wondering.

Why am I here?
Is this what I'm supposed to be doing?

Am I the best caterpillar I can be?

It's tough trying to figure it all out alone.

Fortunately, Yom Kippur is a reminder that we're not all alone.

Even when we can't see Hashem.
Even when we can't feel Hashem.

We're never really alone.
There is a plan for our lives.

On Yom Kippur, we can sometimes start to see what that plan might be.

Become a better caterpillar?
How? I'm pretty great already.

Oh.
That's how.

Change doesn't happen all at once.
That's okay. There's time.

Sometimes it takes a lot of patience.

On Yom Kippur, Hashem helps us start to change.

What's going to happen?

What will my life look like?

For sure, it's going to be full of surprises…

…And I can't wait to see what this new year will bring.

גְּמַר חֲתִימָה טוֹבָה!

G'mar Chatimah Tovah!

May this Yom Kippur be the start of
a year of wonderful changes.

Fold your own Origami Butterfly!

① Start with the colored side up

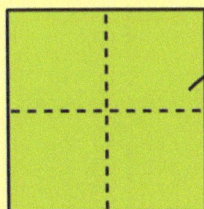

Fold in half both ways. Unfold and turn over

②

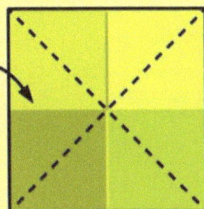

Fold diagonally both ways

③

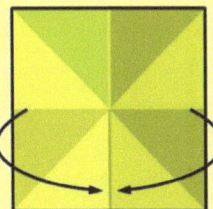

Collapse into triangle shape (see video link for help with this step!)

④

Fold the upper layer only

⑤

Turn over

⑥

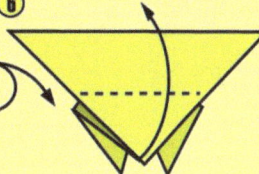

Fold the corner past the edge

⑦

Fold behind. Turn over

⑧

Fold along the center line

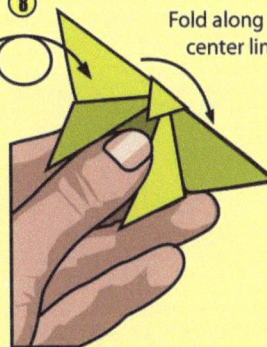

⑨ Pinch the "spine" lightly to help create a nicer shape

* For a helpful video, visit http://tinyurl.com/butterflyfold
Hint: Use colorful paper for more exciting butterflies.

(Try stringing a few together for a lovely Sukkah decoration!)

The Jewish Nature Series:

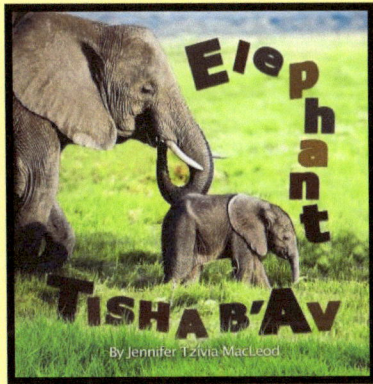

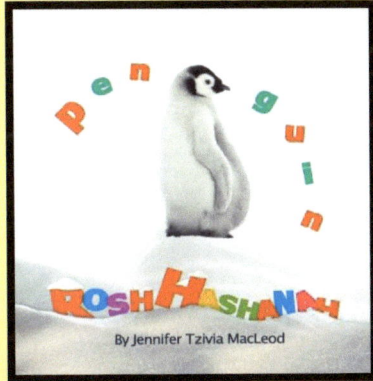

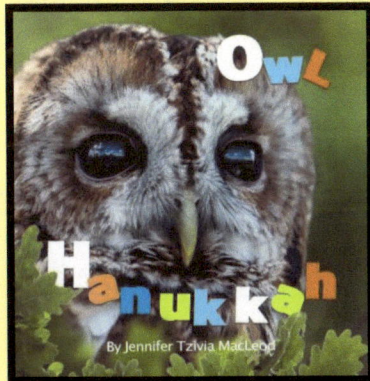

Penguin Rosh Hashanah

Caterpillar Yom Kippur

Turtle Sukkot

Owl Hanukkah

Panda Purim

Otter Passover

Elephant Tisha b'Av

Discover them all at:
http://tinyurl.com/JewishNature

About the Author:

Jennifer Tzivia MacLeod is a proud mother of four (two big and two little), who lives in northern Israel. A freelance writer for magazines and newspapers, she also loves writing stories for her kids and their friends.

Can you help me out?

As an independent children's writer, I count on readers like you who leave feedback for others about my books. If you and your kids liked it, please take a minute to leave a review:

http://tinyurl.com/CaterpillarYom

Thanks! ☺

www.ingramcontent.com/pod-product-compliance
Lightning Source LLC
Chambersburg PA
CBHW041550040426
42447CB00002B/124